Sid the Spe

"Sid, that's my new shoelace!" Vicky said.

But Sid just wanted to play. He leaped over the fluffy slippers on Vicky's feet, and headed for the stairs.

"Sid, give that back! I need that for school!" Vicky yelled.

Sid gave a growl of excitement as he tore down the staircase. "Come and get it, Vicky! This is fun!"

Titles in Jenny Dale's KITTEN TALES™ series

All of Jenny Dale's KITTEN TALES books can
be ordered at your local bookshop or are
available by post from Book Service by Post
(tel: 01624 675137)

Jenny Dale's KITTEN TALES™

Sid the Speedy Kitten

by Jenny Dale

Illustrated by Susan Hellard

A Working Partners Book

MACMILLAN CHILDREN'S BOOKS

To Nathan, who is also speedy!

Special thanks to Gwyneth Rees

First published 2001 by Macmillan Children's Books
a division of Macmillan Publishers Limited
25 Eccleston Place, London SW1W 9NF
Basingstoke and Oxford
www.macmillan.com

Associated companies throughout the world

Created by Working Partners Limited
London W6 0QT

ISBN 0 330 39736 2

1 3 5 7 9 8 6 4 2

A CIP catalogue record for this book is available from
the British Library.

Typeset by SX Composing DTP, Rayleigh, Essex
Printed and bound in Great Britain by Mackays of Chatham plc, Kent

Chapter One

Vicky Nash put both feet
carefully on the floor, and tried to
stand up. But she couldn't stand
without wobbling. She hopped
over to her bedroom door on her
good leg and opened it. "MUM!"
she called out.

"Happy birthday, love!" her

mum called, from halfway up the stairs. "Eight, today!" Mrs Nash's arms were full of parcels and cards.

Vicky's dad was just behind her singing, "Happy birthday to you!" in a very silly voice.

Normally on her birthday Vicky was really excited. But this morning she was more worried about her leg than anything else. Ever since she had broken it she had hoped that it would be better in time for her birthday. So she had been really pleased when the doctor had said she could have her plaster taken off yesterday.

But she couldn't believe how thin and pale her leg looked now. Or how weak it felt when she tried to walk on it. Vicky's physio – the person who helped with exercises to make her leg stronger – had told her that she should try and manage without her crutches.

But Vicky just didn't feel able to try walking without them yet. "Mum, it feels like I'm never going to be able to walk properly again!" she said, plonking back down on the bed.

Vicky's mum put the pile of brightly coloured presents down on the floor. "Vicky, of course you will," she told her firmly. "It's just going to take some time to get back to normal, that's all."

"And you'll be skating around that ice rink again in no time!" her dad added.

Vicky sighed. Ice-skating was
her favourite hobby. The local ice
rink had been booked for her
birthday party this year. Of
course, it had been cancelled
when Vicky had broken her leg.
Vicky's mum and dad had
suggested she have an ordinary
birthday party at home, but Vicky
had been so disappointed that she

didn't want one.

Vicky would have loved to spend her birthday whizzing around on the ice. But even with her plaster off, her leg felt so feeble she couldn't imagine skating ever again. It was a bit scary. "What if—?" she began.

But her dad interrupted her. "What if you open some of these presents?" he said cheerfully. "Or do you want to keep them until you get back from school?"

"Of course I don't!" Vicky said, sounding more like her old self again.

She began to feel excited as her dad passed her the first present. It was from her aunt and uncle – and was beautifully wrapped in bright pink paper.

Vicky ripped it open. Inside was a new tracksuit. She had really wanted one before she broke her leg – and it was perfect. But she couldn't help feeling a little bit disappointed. She didn't need one now.

The next parcel was from Mrs Tippett next door. It was a skipping rope with bright purple handles. Vicky was the best in her class at skipping. But looking at her leg, she didn't think she'd be very good at any games any more.

"No prizes for guessing what this is!" said Mr Nash. He handed Vicky a round parcel, from her Uncle Mark.

"A football," Vicky said, trying not to sound upset. All her presents were lovely – but she couldn't use them!

"And this is from Granny," said her mum. She gave Vicky a big red box tied up with a gold ribbon.

From the way her mum and dad were watching her, Vicky guessed that they thought she was really going to like *this* present.

Her gran had given her a beautiful pair of red leather ice-skates. Vicky felt tears welling up in her eyes. She wanted to go skating again even more now that she had these lovely new skates. But because of her leg, she couldn't!

"Don't you like them?" her mum asked anxiously. "We helped Granny choose them for you. We thought they'd be just what you wanted."

"They would have been," Vicky said sadly, looking down at her leg.

"Don't worry, love. You'll soon be able to use them," said her dad. Then he looked at Vicky's mum and winked. "I won't be long," he said. He went out of the room.

"Where's Dad gone?" Vicky asked.

"To fetch our present to you," said Mrs Nash, smiling. "It's rather special and has to be handled with care!"

Vicky tried to smile back. "What is it?"

Her mum shook her head. "Wait and see," she said.

Vicky looked up as her dad came back into the room. He was carrying a large brown box tied up with a big ribbon. The box had holes punched in the top.

As soon as her dad put the box down on the bed beside her, Vicky heard a scratching noise coming from inside.

Quickly, she untied the ribbon. But before she could open the lid, it was pushed up by a furry little black-and-white head. It was a kitten!

"Meet Sid!" Vicky's dad smiled.

"Sid?" Vicky repeated,

surprised. She said the kitten's
name again, and started to grin.
Sid was a funny, old-fashioned
name. But she liked it!

Hearing his name, the kitten
jumped out of the box and came
over to say hello. Vicky scooped
him up and gave him a cuddle.
Sid began to purr a little.

"Sid was named by his first

owner – a Mr Taylor," Vicky's dad told her. "But poor old Mr Taylor found Sid a bit too lively! He had to take him back to the cat shelter. You can change Sid's name if you want to."

"I don't want to," Vicky said firmly. "I like it. Anyway, he *looks* like a Sid!"

The kitten wriggled free and jumped up onto the dressing table where he inspected himself in the mirror.

"See!" Vicky said. "You *do* look like a Sid, don't you?"

"I certainly do!" Sid miaowed back.

Chapter Two

Sid jumped back onto the bed.

Vicky picked him up again. "At least I can play with *you*, Sid!" she said.

Sid rubbed his face against Vicky's hand. "I'm going to like it here," he purred happily. He loved to be cuddled. But even more than that, he loved to play!

Sid had liked his old home. But he couldn't seem to stop getting under old Mr Taylor's feet. And Mr Taylor used to take naps all the time. He had always wanted to nap just when Sid felt most like playing!

"So let's play, Vicky!" he miaowed. And he jumped out of her arms and buried himself underneath all the wrapping paper. It made a *lovely* crackling noise.

Vicky laughed. She leaned over and chased Sid under the crumpled paper with her hand.

Sid leaped out, and dived onto the floor. "Come on, Vicky!" he mewed. "See if you can catch me!" He started to race round and round the room.

Mrs Nash raised her eyebrows. "Well! He's certainly a very *energetic* kitten," she said.

"Mr Taylor told the cat shelter that even his grandchildren had a job keeping up with Sid!" Vicky's dad said, grinning.

"It's true," Sid agreed, as he

looked around for something to do next. "When Jane and Liam came to visit their grandpa, we had great fun racing round the garden. But they could never catch me!"

Sid had loved playing with Jane and Liam. Kind old Mr Taylor knew that. So he had asked the cat shelter to find a young owner for Sid.

Mr Taylor had then taken Clara home with him. Clara was an old moggie who had been in the shelter for ages. She slept a lot and walked slowly, just like Mr Taylor. Sid was sure that the two of them would get on very well indeed!

*

After breakfast, everyone in the house got ready to go out. Sid felt a bit disappointed when he was put downstairs in the kitchen.

"I'll be back at lunchtime to check Sid's all right," Mrs Nash told Vicky, as she picked up her car keys.

"And *I'll* see you after school, Sid," Vicky called out. "I wish I could stay at home with you all day!"

Sid wished she could too. At least Mr Taylor had been at home with him all day, even if he was asleep in his chair a lot of the time. Still . . . this kitchen was nice and warm. And there was a very tasty bowl of cat food in the corner. And lots of surfaces to jump up onto, and cupboards to investigate. Sid didn't think he'd be too bored, after all.

He went up to the back door and sniffed the garden on the other side of it. Then he jumped up onto the sink and looked out through the window. The garden looked very exciting indeed. Sid

could see big wavy trees and he could hear birds chirping. It was windy and some loose leaves were blowing about on the grass. He couldn't wait to get outside!

When Vicky came home from school, Sid scratched at the back door excitedly. "Come on, Vicky!" he miaowed. "Let's go out."

But Vicky shook her head. "Not yet, Sid," she said. "It's too soon. The cat shelter told us that kittens and cats have to get used to their new home before going outside."

"But I've been getting used to my new home all day! And I don't like waiting for things. I like to do things fast!" Sid mewed miserably. But really, he knew

Vicky was right.

Vicky picked Sid up and gave him a cuddle. "Come on, let's go and play in the living room," she said.

Sid cheered up a bit, and began to purr. "OK," he mewed. "Perhaps I'll have a go at climbing the curtains."

Sid had great fun with his new owner. Vicky played with him and cuddled him all evening. But whenever Sid raced off somewhere, Vicky didn't jump up and run after him. Sid couldn't understand it! Didn't Vicky know how much fun it was to play chasing games?

The next morning, Vicky was

making breakfast. She was balancing on her good leg beside the toaster.

Sid jumped up onto the table to watch the toast pop up. He liked that.

"Down, Sid!" Vicky said, sternly.

Sid pretended he hadn't understood.

"Sid, I said, get down!" Vicky

repeated, hopping over to the table.

Sid moved to the far end. "Oh, are you talking to me?" he mewed innocently.

"Si-id!" Vicky picked up her crutches and started to follow him.

As she reached Sid, he jumped down. "Great!" he miaowed. "You want to play chase!" But then he stopped and sniffed. Something smelled horrible.

Suddenly, the kitchen began to fill with smoke.

"Oh, no!" Vicky yelled. "The toaster's jammed." She hurried back over to the toaster and gave it a tap. Two black slices of toast popped out.

By now, the smoke was making Vicky cough. Without thinking, she went to the back door and opened it to let the smoke out.

Sid couldn't believe his luck! He leaped off the kitchen table and ran out of the door, before Vicky had time to close it again.

"Sid, come back!" Vicky shouted.

But Sid pretended he hadn't heard. At last, he was in the garden!

Chapter Three

Sid ran at the falling leaves,
pouncing on them as they
skimmed across the lawn.
Everything smelled new and
exciting. He spotted an old tree
stump in the middle of the grass,
and climbed on top of it, so he
could get a better view.

A paper bag was dancing in the wind. Sid leaped off the tree stump and ran at top speed to catch it. By this time he was down at the bottom of the garden, far away from the house. He was so excited that he couldn't decide which way to go first.

Then Sid saw the fish pond. Sid *loved* fish! At least, he loved the idea of catching one. Once he had nearly hooked a goldfish out of Mr Taylor's fish pond. Mr Taylor had been very cross with him. And so had the goldfish. Sid had no idea why!

Sid crouched down on his belly so the fish wouldn't see him coming, and crept towards the pond.

Back at the house, Vicky was in a panic. What if Sid ran away and didn't come back? What if he got lost? He was almost out of sight already! Her mum was in the bath, and her dad had already left for work. She would have to go and fetch Sid herself!

Carefully, Vicky used her crutches to get down the back

steps. She could see Sid by the pond. She moved as fast as she could across the grass.

Just as Sid popped a paw into the water, Vicky caught up with him. Quickly, she dropped one crutch to the ground, bent her good leg, and scooped the kitten up. "Got you!" she gasped.

Sid wriggled in surprise. "Hey, Vicky," he miaowed. "I didn't think you would come after me!"

Vicky cuddled her kitten and gave him a kiss. "That was naughty, Sid," she said. But she was smiling.

Sid started to purr. Getting caught was almost as good as running away if it meant you got all this fuss!

As Vicky held Sid tightly, she saw that she couldn't manage to carry Sid back to the house and use both her crutches. *I'll have to leave one behind,* she thought worriedly.

Using only one crutch to support her bad leg, Vicky began to make her way back up the garden. And to her surprise, she managed it quite easily.

She reached the kitchen just as her mum came down the stairs.

"What happened?" Mrs Nash asked, surprised to see Vicky coming in from the garden with Sid.

Vicky told her what had happened. "I don't think I'll take both my crutches to school today," she added as she dropped Sid gently into his basket. "I think I'll be OK with one."

"What a good idea!" Vicky's mum said. She sounded really pleased. And to Sid's surprise, she bent down and stroked him under his chin. "Well done, Sid!" she said.

*

That night, while Vicky was in the bathroom, Sid sat waiting for her. He wished Vicky would hurry up. He thought that having a bath was a very silly thing to do. He couldn't understand why Vicky had to sit in all that water. Why couldn't she just lick herself clean like he did?

Sid decided to sniff the soles of Vicky's shoes to see if he could smell where she'd been today. They smelled as if they'd been to some very interesting places indeed.

Vicky was *still* in the bathroom. So Sid grabbed one of the strings poking out of the shoes. He pulled at it hard. As it came free, the bathroom door opened.

Vicky appeared in the doorway, wrapped in a towel. "Sid, that's my new shoelace!" she said.

But Sid just wanted to play. Dragging the shoelace behind him, he leaped over the fluffy slippers on Vicky's feet, and headed for the stairs.

"Give that back! I need that for school tomorrow!" Vicky yelled.

Sid gave a little growl of excitement as he tore down the staircase. "Come and get it, Vicky! This is fun!"

Vicky hopped across the landing and into her bedroom. She picked up the one crutch that she still used, and started to follow Sid down the stairs.

But she was so slow that by the time she reached the hall he had vanished.

"Mum, did you see Sid rush past? He's taken my shoelace!" Vicky called to her mum, who was in the kitchen.

"No, love," Mrs Nash called back. "He hasn't come in here. Why don't you check the living room? He can't have gone far."

Vicky went to look. But Sid wasn't playing on the fireside rug. And he wasn't on the sofa. Or under it. Suddenly, Vicky heard a noise in the dining room.

When she got there, Vicky saw a bump, halfway up the curtains. The bump looked very kitten-sized . . .

Vicky crept over to the curtains, carefully laid her crutch down on the carpet, and yanked the curtain back.

Sid was sitting on the windowsill with the shoelace looped round one of his ears. "You're getting quite good at this, Vicky!" he mewed.

Vicky grabbed him with both hands. "Sid, you're *so* naughty!"

she said, laughing.

Sid purred loudly. He guessed that must be a good thing. After all, everyone laughed and tickled his tummy when they said it!

A few days later, Sid was sitting on the kitchen windowsill staring longingly out at the garden. He was bored and lonely. Vicky was at school and her mum was out. If only he could go outside and run around!

Just then, Sid spotted Mrs Nash walking up the garden path. She was carrying a huge parcel. Sid wondered if it was another present for Vicky. He jumped down and ran over to the door to say hello.

It took Vicky's mum ages to open the door. And when she did, the parcel slipped to the ground. "Oh, no!" she cried. She bent to pick up the box, leaving the back door wide open.

Sid took his chance. While Mrs Nash was looking the other way, he sped past and hid behind a bush.

Mrs Nash carried in the parcel, laid it on the kitchen table, then went back and closed the door. She didn't seem to have noticed Sid had gone!

Chapter Four

Now that he was outside again, Sid couldn't decide what to do first. Should he find some birds to chase? Or should he have a go at climbing a tree? Then he remembered the fish pond!

He raced down to the bottom of the garden. "Hello!" he mewed to

a shiny orange fish. The fish
swam quickly deeper down into
its pond. Sid couldn't understand
why it didn't seem to like him
very much.

He sat and waited by the side of
the pond for a while. Maybe it
would change its mind and come
up to play.

At last, a flicker of gold came
into sight. Sid put his paw into
the water. But the fish darted
away from him. All Sid caught
was some slimy pondweed.
"You're very good at this game!"
he mewed to the fish. He wiped
the pondweed off onto the grass.

Sid shuffled closer to the side of
the pond and waited again for a
flash of gold to appear.

There it was! He thrust his paw into the water – and missed again. Then further round the pond, another fish came right up to the surface. It stared at Sid cheekily.

Sid whirled round to swipe out at it. But he skidded on the slimy pondweed – and landed, with a loud splash, in the pond!

Just as Sid hit the water, Vicky was walking up the path with her dad. She looked over to see what had made the splash. Sometimes an apple from the nearby tree would drop into the pond, and someone had to lift it out with a net.

Vicky couldn't believe her eyes when she saw her kitten struggling in the water. "SID!" she screamed.

Dropping her crutch at the garden gate, Vicky rushed across the lawn to get to Sid. All she could think about was saving him. Her stiff leg was forgotten.

Sid was very scared. "Save me, Vicky!" he mewed.

Vicky knelt down by the side of

the pond, leaned over, and pulled the kitten out. She hugged him against her even though he was soaking wet. "Oh, Sid!" she cried. "You could have drowned!" She tried to dry him off by rubbing him against her jumper.

Sid let out a faint mew. "Thank you, Vicky," he mewed weakly. He rubbed his little wet head against her. "Perhaps I've played outside enough for today," he added. Then he sneezed.

Vicky's mum rushed down the garden towards them. "What happened? Is that *Sid?*" she asked, looking shocked.

Vicky nodded. "He fell in the pond!"

"Oh! He must have slipped out

when I opened the back door," Mrs Nash cried. "I thought he was asleep upstairs." She reached out to give Sid a stroke. "Poor poppet," she said. "He must have got a terrible fright."

Vicky nodded, still holding Sid close as they all walked up the garden path towards the house.

"Maybe his dip in the water will put him off teasing the fish," said Mr Nash, chuckling.

Vicky nodded, and grinned. "Yes, Sid," she said, giving him another hug. "You were probably being naughty when you fell in! Were you?"

"Sort of," Sid mewed back. He was feeling a bit sorry for himself.

"And another thing, love,"

Mr Nash said, grinning. "You seem to have forgotten this!" He held up the crutch that Vicky had dropped as she rushed to rescue Sid.

"Vicky!" her mum cried. "Did you get all the way up the garden without using your crutch?"

Vicky nodded. "I didn't even think about it!" she explained.

"Well, look how well you're walking without it!" Mrs Nash said proudly. "All that rushing around after Sid must be helping your leg get stronger."

Sid's ears pricked up. What was this? Rushing around after him was a *good* thing for Vicky? Well, in that case . . . Sid made up his mind that he was going to *really* speed up from now on!

Chapter Five

Now that she had tried it, Vicky felt able to walk without her crutch. But she was still scared to put her whole weight on her bad leg. She didn't play football with her friend Kevin – or do gym at school. And even though Vicky really missed it, she didn't try ice-skating, either.

But at least she had Sid to keep her busy. He seemed to speed around the house even more now. Vicky had to work hard to keep up with him!

The day soon arrived when Sid was allowed outside on his own. Vicky's mum had bought him a special collar with a little bell on it. Sid tried to tell her that a bell was a nuisance when you wanted to chase birds, but he couldn't seem to make her understand. He had his own name-tag too. It had SID written on it in big letters, and the Nashes' telephone number on the back.

But when Vicky opened the

back door and carried Sid out onto the patio, he forgot all that! He sniffed the air, wondering where to explore first.

Suddenly, Sid noticed something moving in a heap of fallen leaves by the hedge. "Put me down, Vicky!" he mewed, wriggling in her arms.

Vicky grinned and let Sid jump to the ground.

Sid almost fell over himself in his rush to get there. He raced over to the hedge and threw himself at the pile of leaves. But for once, Sid was too slow. A squirrel darted out. It scurried away up a tree trunk to the safety of the leafy branches above.

Sid made a crash landing. He

tumbled over and over in the golden leaves.

"You're not very speedy, are you?" the squirrel chattered at him cheekily. "My grandma could do better than that!"

Sid was *very* offended. He tried to growl fiercely, but it came out as a squeak. "Come here and say that again!"

"Come and get me!" chattered the squirrel. He swished his bushy tail from side to side, then dropped an acorn. It landed on Sid's nose.

"Right!" Sid hissed. "You asked for it!" He leaped onto the trunk of the tree and began to climb.

"Sid!" called Vicky, sounding alarmed.

"It's OK, Vicky," Sid mewed
back. "I'm just going to teach this
cheeky squirrel a lesson. Won't be
long." Sid struggled onto the
lowest branch. Then up to the
next. And the next . . .

Sid was almost there. He
couldn't wait to take a swipe at
that cheeky squirrel's tail.

But suddenly, the squirrel

leaped down onto the same branch as Sid. "Watch out!" he squeaked.

Sid nearly lost his balance as the branch wobbled horribly. He looked down – and froze. The ground seemed a *very* long way away!

"Poor kitty!" chirruped the squirrel. "See you later!" And he leaped down onto another branch, scampered along it, then darted back down the tree trunk.

Sid was stuck. And scared. He could see Vicky looking up at him, with a worried look on her face. "Help me, Vicky!" he mewed.

"It's OK, Sid!" Vicky called up to him. "If you got up there, you can get down again. Just take your time!"

But Sid wasn't so sure about that. He stayed right where he was, digging his claws in as hard as he could.

Vicky moved from foot to foot, wondering what to do. She would have to climb the tree if she was going to rescue her kitten.

Before she'd broken her leg, Vicky had climbed loads of trees with Kevin. But what if her leg still wasn't strong enough for her to climb on it? What if it broke again? The doctor said she could do anything she wanted to now. But Vicky was still scared.

Sid mewed again, much louder

this time.

Vicky looked up at Sid and made up her mind. "It's OK, Sid. I'm coming!" she called. Her heart beating fast, she reached up and grabbed hold of the lowest branch.

Vicky put her good leg firmly against the tree trunk and pushed herself up. Then she held her breath, shifted her weight onto her bad leg – and pushed. All her weight was on that leg now. But it didn't give way. It didn't even feel wobbly! Vicky let out a sigh of relief.

She moved one arm to grab a higher branch and hauled herself further up. Soon, Sid was almost within reach. One more step up, and Vicky was level with him.

She scooped Sid up and he clung tightly to her sweatshirt with his claws. "Don't look down, Vicky," he mewed. "It's very scary!"

Now Vicky had to climb down again. But luckily, Sid was clinging on so tightly, she didn't have to carry him. With both hands free, Vicky soon had them back on the ground.

Sid started to purr loudly. He was safe again! "Thanks, Vicky! I knew you could do it!" He was so happy, he wanted to race around. He jumped out of Vicky's arms and zoomed across the lawn.

Vicky laughed and laughed. She had climbed a tree again! And if

she could climb trees then her leg *really was* completely better! She felt so happy that she started to race round the garden too. "Wait for me, Sid!" she called.

Now that Vicky's leg was back to normal the only thing left to do was try out her new ice-skates. And she had an idea about that . . .

"Mum, how about me having a sort of *belated* birthday party at the ice-rink?" she asked the next morning, at breakfast.

Mrs Nash smiled. "That's just what I was thinking, love," she said. "I'll phone up and re-book it for you!"

When Vicky wasn't looking,

Mrs Nash stroked Sid and whispered, "Thanks for helping Vicky get better, Sid."

But Sid didn't hear her. He was fast asleep, dreaming of chasing squirrels.

Snuggles the Sleepy Kitten

Snuggles loves sleeping. In his dreams, Snuggles is brave and wild – just like a tiger. He can even chase dogs!

But Mark, who lives next door, wants a kitten to play with. Can he persuade sleepy Snuggles to stay awake?

Pip the Prize Kitten

John loves his new kitten, Pip. He thinks she's beautiful. But the posh pedigree cats she lives with don't think so. They say she'll never win "best cat" prizes, like they do.

Pip's already a winner for John. But is it true that only posh pets win prizes?

Collect all of JENNY DALE'S KITTEN TALES™!

The prices shown below are correct at the time of going to press. However, Macmillan Publishers reserve the right to show new retail prices on covers which may differ from those previously advertised.

JENNY DALE'S KITTEN TALES™

1.	Star the Snow Kitten	0 330 37451 6	£2.99
2.	Bob the Bouncy Kitten	0 330 37452 4	£2.99
3.	Felix the Fluffy Kitten	0 330 37453 2	£2.99
4.	Nell the Naughty Kitten	0 330 37454 0	£2.99
5.	Leo the Lucky Kitten	0 330 37455 9	£2.99
6.	Patch the Perfect Kitten	0 330 37456 7	£2.99
7.	Lucy the Lonely Kitten	0 330 37457 5	£2.99
8.	Colin the Clumsy Kitten	0 330 37458 3	£2.99
9.	Poppy the Posh Kitten	0 330 39733 8	£2.99
10.	Snuggles the Sleepy Kitten	0 330 39734 6	£2.99
11.	Pip the Prize Kitten	0 330 39735 4	£2.99
12.	Sid the Speedy Kitten	0 330 39736 2	£2.99

All Macmillan titles can be ordered at your local bookshop or are available by post from:

Book Service by Post
PO Box 29, Douglas, Isle of Man IM99 1BQ

Credit cards accepted. For details:
Telephone: 01624 675137
Fax: 01624 670923
E-mail: bookshop@enterprise.net

Free postage and packing in the UK.
Overseas customers: add £1 per book (paperback)
and £3 per book (hardback).